T0195790

Tephi's Sacred Journey

N.P. SEARLE

BALBOA.PRESS

A DIVISION OF HAY HOUSE

Balboa Press books may be ordered through booksellers or by contacting:

Balboa Press
A Division of Hay House
1663 Liberty Drive
Bloomington, IN 47403
www.balboapress.com
1 (877) 407-4847

Because of the dynamic nature of the Internet, any web addresses or links contained in this book may have changed since publication and may no longer be valid. The views expressed in this work are solely those of the author and do not necessarily reflect the views of the publisher, and the publisher hereby disclaims any responsibility for them.

The author of this book does not dispense medical advice or prescribe the use of any technique as a form of treatment for physical, emotional, or medical problems without the advice of a physician, either directly or indirectly. The intent of the author is only to offer information of a general nature to help you in your quest for emotional and spiritual well-being. In the event you use any of the information in this book for yourself, which is your constitutional right, the author and the publisher assume no responsibility for your actions.

Any people depicted in stock imagery provided by Getty Images are models, and such images are being used for illustrative purposes only. Certain stock imagery © Getty Images.

Print information available on the last page.

ISBN: 978-1-9822-4102-5 (sc)
ISBN: 978-1-9822-4104-9 (hc)
ISBN: 978-1-9822-4103-2 (e)

Library of Congress Control Number: 2020900351

Balboa Press rev. date: 04/15/2020

Acknowledgments

James Munford for his vision and insight of bringing
Tephi and the magical world she lives in into reality

Ingrid Smith and Linda Kurtenbach for spending
so much time and energy in editing waking song,
Marlis A Simms-Delaronde for her time and energy in
editing the Four Winds and The Teachings of Tephi

Aliah Tedjmulia for the voice for the song and
lyrics translated in the Atlantean language

Adrienne Read for bringing the magic
to the song with flute and piccolo

Jonathan Searle, my brother, for his work
brining the book from dream to reality

And all of family and friends who have supported
me through the journey of this book.

Dedicated to

All of those that have brought this story into reality

Once upon a time in a land not too far from yours lived a fairy named Tephi. She had short, brown hair resembling that of a bluebell flower. Her eyes held every brilliant color of the rainbow. She stood no taller than a toad stool and was beautiful and pale as the full moon. Even though she was not aware of it, Tephi had a very unique gift: She could make plants grow by singing.

See, as she would walk and sing, every flower she passed bloomed, all trees' leaves budded and unfolded, and where she stepped, new grass grew.

The plants all knew Tephi's voice was magic, but Tephi didn't know this.

One day, as Tephi fluttered up a stream bed from stone to stone, she saw a great oak in the distance she hadn't noticed before. The great oak's branches reached up past the sky. The brown bark was coarse and rough, and it stood in the middle of a field of lush green grass. With a few hops and with a flutter of her wings, she stood at the base of the great oak.

She placed her hand on the great oak and asked, "Great oak, what wonders have you seen in your many years? What stories do you have to tell?"

As Tephi stood there connecting with the tree, a menacing dark cloud started to move in, covering up the sun. Soon, the dark cloud let out a big

BOOOOOOM and then a ccrraasshh.
Lightning lit up the sky.

Because Tephi never had been so far from home and never had been out in a storm as windy and wet as this one, the lightning and thunder sent chills down her little spine. She looked around, and under a shrub she saw her friend, Henry the rabbit.

Henry was the fastest rabbit in those parts of the woods. Everyone knew Henry by the white patch of fur between his eyes that resembled a star. It let him see ten steps ahead of where he was going. Others say it was because he was gray from the tip of his ears to the tip of his toes. The true reason why he was the fastest, however, was because Henry just knew he was. Henry was lying on the ground, his paws over his eyes.

Tephi saw that he was scared. She walked over to Henry and placed her small hand on the star. After that, Henry stopped shaking. He uncovered his eyes and looked at Tephi, knowing the comfort her touch brought.

Tephi whispered in his ear, "Henry, I know you're scared and so am I. I need to get back to the village. I need your courage and speed, my dear friend."

With that, Henry lowered his ears, nodded for Tephi to climb on, and with the next crash of lightning, they bolted off.

Looking back, Tephi saw the lightning hit the great oak. The great oak cried out, "Ttteeeepppppphhhhiiii." Soon, it was engulfed in flames and was burning to the forest floor.

Henry, carrying them as fast as his feet could take them, sprinted quickly to the edge of the village. Henry lowered his head. As Tephi climbed off, she wrapped her arms around his neck and said, "Thank you, my brave friend."

Puzzled, Tephi flew into the village. "Did the great oak call out my name? No, I must have been imagining it… or was I? Can trees really talk?"

"I have to find someone who can shed some light on this. I know. I'll go see the elders. They'll have the answers", she said aloud to herself.

In her search for answers, she made her way to the hall where the elders met to discuss secrets and knowledge.

Tephi burst into the hall, and a hush fell over the elders. Their gaze focused on her. "Yes, child," one asked, "what do you seek?"
Tephi stepped forward and humbly asked, "Elders, can trees talk?"
They looked at each other and started to laugh. "No, child, trees cannot talk. Why would you ask such a question?"
Tephi replied, somewhat withdrawn, "When I was in the storm, I saw a great oak get struck by lightning, and I thought it called out my name."
Again, the elders broke out in laughter. After their laughter quieted, another spoke, "Tephi, those are stories that have been told from childhood, stories our ancestors passed down on how at one time they were able to talk with trees, stones, and flowers. But they are just stories, stories to excite your imagination."

With that, Tephi left the hall not feeling
satisfied with the answer the elders gave and
being very dissapointed. She knew, deep down
in her heart, that the tree had called her name.
She asked herself, "Where do I turn now?"

While her wings carried her through
the village, Tephi felt lost.

She said, "I asked the wisest elders, and they
laughed at me. Who has the answers if the wise
elders don't know. Whom do I ask now?"
The wind spoke with a gust, "Dunkelwison."
Startled, Tephi looked around and
asked, "Who said that?"
There was no one around. Puzzled, thinking she must
have imagined it, she repeated, "Whom do I ask now?"
The wind gusted again, "Dunkelwison."
Tephi asked, "Who is Dunkelwison?
Where do I find him?"
The wind answered, "Go to the hill that overlooks
your village. There you will find a stone with an
old-looking face. Over the years, the moss that has
grown has become his beard. A condor's nest sits
on top of his head and has become his hair. He is
very wise and holds the answer to your question."

"There are a lot of hills that overlook our village. How will I find the one where Dunkelwison is?" Tephi asked overwhelmed.

The wind answered, "Your heart knows. Follow your heart, Tephi."

Tephi closed her eyes and decided to listen to the wind's advice, so she could follow her heart.

After turning in a half circle, Tephi had a feeling to stop. When she opened her eyes, she saw the hill where she would find Dunkelwison. She flew to the top of the hill, and on it was a lone stone. The moss had grown thick around the base of it, giving the stone the appearance of a beard. Up on the top was the nest of a condor that resembled a hairdo of someone who had just awakened from a long slumber. The eyes were closed.

Tephi started to whisper,
"Dunkelwison? Dunkelwison?"
When there was no answer, she flew to the
top of the stone and sat on the nest.
After several minutes, Tephi said,
"Is this the right place?"

Just then, a rumbling started, and
the rock began to move.
Dunkelwison awoke.
"OOOOHHHHHHH MY MY MYYYYYYY.
Who is sitting atop my head?"

Tephi jumped and fluttered to where she
was face to face with Dunkelwison.
"My name is Tephi," she said timidly,
not knowing what to expect.
"Hmmmm," Dunkelwison blinked his eyes, "Come
closer, Tephi. Let me get a good look at you. I haven't
seen a fairy for a long time, let alone spoke to one."
Tephi asked hesitantly, "Are you Dunkelwison?"
The rock smiled, replying, "Yes, Tephi.
That is what I am known as."
Tephi returned the smile, saying, "I was
told to come see you, Dunkelwison."
"Hmmm, by whom might I ask?"
Tephi looked away, sharing, "By the wind."
"Hmmm, very interesting. A fairy
that can talk with the wind?"
Tephi answered. "Yes, no, I, I think so, Dunkelwison."
Dunkelwison was intrigued. "Tell me more,
Tephi. What brought you to me?"
Tephi retold the whole story of the great
oak and how it was struck by lightning and
how she thought it called out her name.

When she finished, Dunkelwison said, "Not in many years has someone been able to talk with us: the earth, the trees, the wind. You are very special, Tephi. You must have a very special gift. The answer that you seek will be revealed to you. Make your way back to where the great oak stood. There, you will know your answer and the nature of your gift.

Satisfied with his answer, Tephi thanked Dunkelwison and started back to where the great oak stood.

Carried off by her wings, Tephi thought, I wonder what the answer will be and what my gift is. I don't think I have a gift.

Her little wings grew tired as she reached the great oak. She was shocked when she found that only a burnt black stump remained.

Somewhat at a loss, Tephi wondered, "what am I supposed to do?" She looked around and asked, "what do I do now?"

She was not aware that the wind had been her constant companion until it replied, "Stand in the middle of the great oak's stump."

Flying to the center of the charred stump, Tephi closed her eyes and felt the great oak still there. She knelt down, placed both hands on the center ring of the stump, and had a feeling to open her mouth. As she did, a song came out!

"After the fire comes the rain.
Grow, grow, grow again.
Wake from your slumber. Time to rise.
Grow, grow, grow again.
I see the beauty that you'll be.
Grow, grow, grow again.
Love from my heart to yours you'll see.
Grow, grow, grow again.

After the winter, spring does come.
Grow, grow, grow again.
Stretch forth your roots and rise above.
Grow, grow, grow again.
I see the beauty that you'll be.
Grow, grow, grow again.
Love from my heart to yours you'll see.
Grow, grow, grow again."

Singing this song with her eyes closed, Tephi could feel new sprouts start to rise from the burnt stump. As they grew taller and taller, they swirled around Tephi, enclosing her as part of the new tree. Once again, it stood as the great oak it once was.

With autumn dropping its leaves, winter's white snow faded, and spring brought new leaves. The first green leaf as it unfolded held a small fairy.

In it was Tephi...

The Four Winds

Stretching her arms and with a big yawn Tephi awakened on the leaf of the full grown oak. She looked down at herself and saw that something was different. Her clothes were different, they were a brilliant color of purple. She flapped her wings as she descended to the base of the oak.

She stood on the roots of the tree and looked up in wonder at what had just happened. "Was I inside of the oak? Why do I have different clothes? Why does it feel like it's spring now?" She thought to herself. So many questions entered her mind but at the same time she felt at peace and connected with the earth more than ever.

She reached out and touched the oak. The rough coarse bark that she had noticed before wasn't rough, it was smooth as glass and when the light hit the oak it shimmered. Placing her hands on the oak, she thanked it for the connection they had made. While doing this the tree started to bow and the wind shook its leaves.

Questions raced through Tephi's mind. "I need to know what has just happened. I know Dunkelwison will help me make sense of all of this." With that she started to flap her wings lightly and lifted up off the ground. As she flew to Dunkelwison she noticed something different. The land seemed more alive the air felt more freeing. Plants, trees and flowers seemed to have a truer more brilliant color to them that she hadn't noticed before.

Making her way out of the woods, she saw Dunkelwison in a restful state. She flew in front of him and landed on the piece of rock that was his nose. Tephi spoke his name softly, "Dunkelwison...Dunkelwison... Dunkelwison..." with that Dunkelwison slowly awoke blinking his eyes.

"Ohhhhhh my dear Tephi." As he focused his eyes towards the end of his nose he spoke. "fly out a little ways so I can get a better look at you."

Tephi fluttered out about ten feet from his nose.

"Oh look at you. Something is different. Your clothing, wherever did you receive that?"

Tephi answered, "I don't know? I think the oak gave it to me."

Dunkelwison answered, "Your intuition is correct dear one. Tell me Tephi, did you find out what your gift is?"

"I think so." She replied. "It's a song."

"Oh," stated Dunkelwison. "Tell me how you received this song."

Tephi answered. "Well, as I flew back to the oak all I saw was a burnt stump. I flew to the center, kneeled down and placed my hands at the center. It's funny, although it was burnt I could feel it very much alive. I heard a song that was being sung to me and as I opened my mouth to sing could feel the roots growing out and down through the earth, absorbing the water and nutrients. I felt new stems sprout up around me and within seconds I was wrapped up in them becoming part of the tree. So near the heart of it."

Dunkelwison smiled. "While you were near its heart what did you notice?"

"I don't know. I don't remember." Tephi replied.

Dunkelwison spoke softly. "Close your eyes dear one. Being near to the oak's heart what did you notice? What did you learn from its heart?"

Tephi closed her eyes and searched back into her thoughts and memories. "I was connected to it, but not just to the oak, I was connected to everything. I could feel the wind blow through the leaves and its branches. I could hear the rain splashing on the ground, and felt its renewing power. I could taste the richness of the earth through its roots. Beyond that I sensed a stream in the distance running over the rocks and very deep down below the oak there was a cavern. A cavern that is very unique and special. I learned how very connected I am with this world."

Remembering, Tephi opened her eyes, and saw Dunkelwison smiling at her.

"Yes child, you have learned one of the most beautiful lessons of this life. Indeed we are all connected in more ways than we know. A time will come when you'll share and teach this lesson to others accompanied with the song. You will show your kind what they have forgotten."

Tephi smiled feeling at peace. She asked, "What about the cavern I felt below the oak?"

Dunkelwison answered. "That is a story for another time of another's journey. Now is your time. Are you ready for the next part of your journey Tephi?"

Feeling more confident in herself Tephi flew up to Dunkelwison and said. "Yes, Dunkelwison. I am."

Dunkelwison smiled and started to open his mouth, a very low rumbling started "AAAAAAHHHHHHHHHHHHHH." It continued to grow louder and deeper till the earth shook and the trees bowed.

Soon a giant condor started to take shape in the sky and circled the area where Dunkelwison was creating the low tone. Upon landing, its massive wings pushed the air beneath it to land comfortably sending Tephi tumbling head over heels. As the condor sat atop Dunkelwisons head, Dunkelwison began to speak, "Tephi this is a very old and kind friend. He is called Starlious, he will assist you to the place of your birth."

Somewhat intimidated, Tephi flew up to Starlious. Dunkelwison spoke. "Fly up around his shoulders, you should travel nicely among his feathers on his shoulders." Tephi fluttered to where the shoulder met Starlious' neck and nestled herself under a few feathers.

"Safe travels Tephi I look forward to seeing you again." Dunkelwison said. With that the giant condor spread its wings and with a couple whooshes from its gigantic wings they were off. Circling ever upward until Tephi could no longer see the ground.

Flying higher and higher up she clung tightly onto the feathers between her tiny hands. In the distance there started to appear a mountain peak surrounded by clouds. As they flew closer Tephi could see there was a flat area with lush green grass and moss covered rocks that stood in a circle. Flapping its wings downward Starlious descended gracefully till he and Tephi landed in the center of the circle of rocks.

Tephi released her tight grip and flew off Starlious's back. With a great flap of his wings Starlious took off up into the sky. She fluttered around looking at the stones that were partially covered in moss. She could see some engravings upon the stones peeking from under parts of the moss. Tephi fluttered up to the engravings to get a closer look. "Fairies!" She exclaimed. "They're fairies!" Examining each stone column she looked thinking to herself. "What do these carvings have to do with me? With my kind?" Flying around she noticed stones missing in each of the four directions and a circular flat stone lying in the center of the green grass between them.

She flew from column to column and noticed more of the same engravings of fairies. They were standing in the center of the stone with the four directions facing them. She thought to herself. "What does this mean?" She asked aloud. "What does this mean?"

While asking this she looked up and noticed a great funnel cloud start to swirl around until the tip of the cloud touched the center stone and split it into four wispy ever moving clouds slowly taking form.

"Tephi come to the center of us." The first said that was from the most northern direction. Tephi fluttered over to the center of the four winds lightly landing on the center stone.

The north wind spoke. "An introduction is in order. I am Grelos the wind of the north."

The east wind spoke. "I am Syllydidy the wind of the east." Next the south wind spoke. "I am Delariah the wind of the south." Then the west spoke. "I am Tulamar the wind of west."

Tephi answered in a humble voice, "I am Tephi."

"We know dear one." The four spoke as one. Grelos spoke. "It seems that you have some questions Tephi." Tephi nodded.

Syllydidy stated. "Ask them, for we cannot answer that which you do not ask."

Tephi thought for a while and asked. "I was flying around here and I noticed the columns have fairies on them. And the four directions. What does this mean?"

Delariah answered. "It is here where you were given life. As well as everyone of your kind. This is where you came into existence. The 4 directions are where we take our place. We place each new fairy in the center. Grelos and I breathe life into you while Tulamar and Syllydidy give lift to your wings."

Tears of gratitude welled up in her eyes knowing where she was from and meeting her makers.

"Thank you." Tephi said gratefully. She thought some more. "There are no stories of this place in our history books. How is it that none of my kind remember our birth?"

$\mathcal{T}$ulamar answered. "There are only a few we have entrusted with this sacred knowledge. You know one of them."

Tephi spoke softly. "Dunkelwison."

"You are correct." Said Tulamar. "Long ago when the wind, earth, water, and fire were creating this world and the inhabitants on it, we knew the day would come that those whom we had created would lose their way. So we placed certain ancestors in places to guide the communication of our creation back to us."

Tephi asked. "Is Starlious the only way to get to this place?"

relos answered. "Yes, Starlious is the only way to get to this place. We taught Dunkelwison the sacred sound that would call him down from the cosmos. Only by the sacred sound that Dunkelwison can sing and through the flight of Starlious can you be here."

Tephi thought some more, and asked. "You mentioned that my kind has lost their way. What do you mean by that?"

Syllydidy answered. "Your kind has fallen more into material desires. That wasn't what you were created for. Your kind are the stewards of this planet. You were created to see past what is in front of you and bring out the truth and beauty in nature. That is all your kinds' gifts. That is why we taught you the first song of many that will cause you to bring life. Bringing forth even life from death.

Tephi asked. "You were the voices I heard that led me to Dunkelwison, and taught me the song?"

All four answered. "Yes dear one."

Tephi thought for a split second. "Why did you choose me?"

Delariah answered. "Because long before we gave you the song you were already singing. Bringing beauty everywhere you flew. That is why you are chosen."

Humbled, Tephi thanked the four and she asked. "What do I do now?"

Tulamar answered. "There will come a time in the near future when you will teach your kind what you have learned."

Tephi politely interrupted. "I can't teach, last time I asked a question the elders laughed at my inquiry. How can I teach those who are wiser than me?"

Grelos answered. "You will teach that which you've learned, by doing so you teach truer wisdom from us. The time is close at hand when your kind will be even more lost. Already set into motion a winged friend has been on his journey and this is his last task to perform. You are already needed Tephi. Trust us, your kinds' hearts will be open to your teachings."

Tephi feeling overwhelmed said. "I don't know if I can do this."

"Let go of the fears and worries, we are always with you dear one." The four spoke as one.

With that the four started to swirl together like an upside down tornado until they became one and disappeared again from whence they came.

Feeling a little more secure knowing that the four were always with her, Tephi asked. "How do I get home from here?"

The wind answered, "You know how to call Starlious."

Tephi closed her eyes, opened her mouth and started to sing. "Aaaahhhhh." She opened her eyes while looking up she could see something starting to take shape and pretty soon she saw Starlious circling down to where she was. She clung to the nearest shrub as its massive wings flapped to slow himself down. When he landed Tephi flew up where she had nestled down before and gripped the closest feathers. Starlious took off. Soon they were circling ever upward and the mountain peak disappeared out of sight.

Descending she saw a shape flying through the clouds. Although she couldn't be sure, she swore it was in the shape of a dragon.

Peering through the clouds she could see her village. Nothing was out of the ordinary from what she could see. She thought back to what Grelos said. "How will my kind be even more lost? How will I get them to listen to me? How will their hearts be opened?" As Tephi thought these questions Starlious landed on the nest atop Dunkelwison.

Tephi released her grip and flew face to face with Starlious. Tephi placed her tiny forehead against Starlious' giant forehead, and placed her hands over her heart and not a word was spoken.

After a few minutes, Starlious started flapping his wings and took off back up to the cosmos.

Tephi flew down to see Dunkelwison smiling at her. He spoke gently. "Tell me Tephi what did you learn?"

With tears in her eyes she spoke, "I learned where I'm from and what our purpose is here."

Dunkelwison responded. "And what is your purpose Tephi?"

"I am to teach my kind what I've learned. That we've forgotten we are the caretakers of this world and our voices are magic. We each have the power to make things grow." Tephi answered

Dunkelwison smiled then said. "Indeed you and your kind are. The winds have chosen a very special creation as a teacher." He smiled at Tephi, as he did she flew up and gave him a tiny hug on his big nose.

The Teachings of Tephi

A long time ago in a land not too far from yours…

A young fairy and her friend, the rock, were talking.

"Dunkelwison, i'm still a little nervous about teaching my kind, let alone the elders." Tephi said.

"What did the winds tell you?" Dunkelwison asked. Tephi answered with a gleam of light sparkling in her eye. "That they are always with me, to let go of my fears and worries. They also talked about a winged friend to them that was on his journey, I still don't understand who he is."

Dunkelwison spoke. "All in due time as we speak he is on his way to your village to help your kind open their hearts up to you."

Tephi looked at Dunkelwison. "Open their hearts up to me?" Tephi said confused. Dunkelwison replied. "Yes my dear Tephi you'll see. Focus on your journey, soon enough you will understand and greet each other."

Tephi smiled and spoke. "Thank you Dunkelwison for all that you have done." Dunkelwison replied. "You are very welcome my dear Tephi. It is time for you to start back to your village you are needed there."

Tephi flew up and gave Dunkelwison a hug on his big rocky nose, then turned and started to flutter off back to her village.

The sky grew dark as she looked up she saw in the clouds an image that blotted out the sun. Can it be she thought to herself? Is that a dragon? As soon as it appeared it was gone again. She turned to Dunkelwison just off in the distance, she fluttered in one place looking at him as if to ask what she had just seen was a dragon. She could see Dunkelwison smile. "Yes my dear it was a dragon hurry, your village needs you."

She turned smiling and as fast as she could flap her wings she was off. While she was flying so many thoughts raced through her mind. Who is the other I will meet? How will I teach the others? I'm not that old or wise unlike the elders.

Then remembering when she had asked them about the wind and them laughing at her question. Her train of thought was interrupted when she heard a voice saying. "Faster Tephi, faster your village needs you." The wind gusted. Tephi spoke. "I'm flying as fast as I can."

The wind spoke. "We know you are flying as fast as your mind will let you. Let us help."

Tephi responded. "Thank you." With that she took a deep breath and started to flap her little wings even harder. With a word from the wind on a small breeze that kissed Tephi's wings she was gone from the visible sight of normal eyes.

All of a sudden she felt as though she wasn't flapping at all. She looked at her wings and there was a new set that had emerged and was flapping along with her others. She couldn't believe her eyes.

She asked the wind as she continued flapping towards her village. "What are these?"

The wind answered. "These are your true wings, the wings that we have given to all our creation. try flapping them faster."

Flapping her new wings faster, Tephi felt how effortless she could glide on the wind. Changing the color of her body to a brilliant mystic blue. She had arrived at the edge of her village within mere seconds only to see it engulfed in flames.

As she slowed her wings down to a normal flutter, she came back into sight. Tephi landed on a nearby branch that overlooked her village. She watched with bewilderment as her fairy village was burning to the ground.

She saw fairies throwing buckets of water on the fire trying to put it out, working frantically to keep their possessions and old shelters.

Something caught her eye down on the ground that wasn't flying. It was a salamander. She watched it continue to crawl from tree to tree and shelter to shelter. Breathing fire while opening its mouth. But it wasn't a fire she had seen before. Unlike the yellow and red flames we are used to seeing, the fire coming out of the salamander's mouth was a deep purple, that one would only see in the deepest depths of the ocean and the brightest blue that resides in the highest parts of the sky. It really was a beautiful flame.

The salamander lit the last tree that held the shelter in the village, it turned to see the fire and as it burned he looked up to the branch that Tephi was crouched upon. He smiled and as he did wings started to grow the color of a crimson red. He started to flap them and with each flap he grew in size and as his wings grew his tail started to shoot out growing longer and his neck stretched towards the sky. Soon the whole dragon was back to full size blotting out the sun. The wind from its wings fanned the flames burning the village to the ground.

Turning to leave he looked at Tephi once more, made eye contact, smiled and flew high up into the sky until he disappeared from view.

Tephi looked back to the village as everything was burning to the ground: trees, shrubs, shelters many of the fairies were on the outskirts watching their homes burn, all memories fading as the deep purple and brightest blue flames consumed everything. Some fairies watched with tears in their eyes as the flames burned into the night.

When the first rays of light hit what was once a village all that was there was ash and a few cinders floating on the breeze giving their last light.

Tephi looked around where the village had once stood, saddened by the loss of her fellow fairies, as they fluttered around rummaging through the remains of the ashes only to find there was nothing that remained.

Tephi so wanted to help, as she fluttered to the center of the cindered city. She cleared her throat and said. "I can help." A few of the fairies looked at her and when they saw it was Tephi quickly looked away again and continued to rummage through the ashes desperately looking for a single piece of their old life.

Tephi spoke louder. "I CAN HELP." She noticed everyone stopped and looked at her. And one asked. "How can you help Tephi?"

Finding a tree that was nearby she placed her hands in the center on the stump. As she started to sing her voice cracked and she looked up to see all eyes were on her. So she started to sing again, her little voice cracked once more as she started to hear murmurs from the other fairies.

"What is she trying to do?" One said. "How is this helping any of us?" Another whispered One by one they turned back sifting through the ashes.

Tephi got up off her knees and fluttered slowly up to the edge of the village where the trees and shrubs grew thick. She disappeared into the undergrowth saddened with what had just happened.

"What happened?" She thought as she continued to fly in no particular direction. "Why didn't it work? What did I do wrong?" The thoughts of doubt crept into her mind. She continued till she came to a place that looked vaguely familiar as if she had been in this meadow behind a rock like this She flew up higher and she noticed a few sticks that then made a nest. "Oh." She thought. "Dunkelwison!"

"Hello Tephi." Dunkelwison spoke. Tephi replied. "How did you know I was here?"

"Well my dear, I've always been able to hear fairies, but only when they are in their true state. Fly around here so I may see you." Dunkelwison said.

Tephi flew around. She noticed a little path that led to a small cave on the side of Dunkelwision's head as if he had an ear.

She made her way to the front and saw laying down in the grass before Dunkelwison the beautiful dragon that had burnt down her village. Hesitantly she continued to fly forward to see Dunkelwison.

Dunkelwison spoke. "Hello Tephi, it's so good to see you." Tephi was nervous she opened her mouth to reply but no words came out just a tiny squeak like a mouse.

Dunkelwison smiled. "Forgive me Tephi, I haven't introduced you to my friend. This is Eliho."

Tephi flew close to Dunkelwison and whispered. "I think he is the one that burned down my village."

Dunkelwison spoke. "I know Tephi." Looking puzzled she whispered? "Why did he do it?"

Dunkelwison kindly whispered. "Well my dear Tephi he's right here, why don't you ask him? Be brave little one."

ustering up her courage, Tephi flew so she was face to face with Eliho the Dragon. Her little voice cracking as she spoke to the massive dragon.

"Excuse me sir." She stammered.

Eliho sighed letting out some clear white smoke from his nostrils. Then gazing into Tephis eyes she sensed a feeling of peace come over her now that she was being more calm she asked. "Was it you who burned down my village?"

Eliho closed his eyes and lowered his head as if bowing to Tephi then replied. "Yes child."

Tephi asked in a somber voice. "Why?"

Eliho raised his head back up so he was looking back into her eye and replied. "Because child, that is my gift."

Confused, Tephi turned her head to look at Dunkelwison. Only to see him smiling.

She turned back to Eliho. "Gift?" She said questioning. "How is burning a village down a gift?"

Eliho stood up and then with a big deep inhale of his breath he stood up on his hind legs opening his wings Tephi saw where his heart was it started to glow changing color from purple to blue and back again until he let out a big roar and what followed was the brilliant blue and purple flames heading straight for Tephi.

Tephi, not having time to react was overtaken by the flame as it passed straight through her until Elihos breath subsided. She was still fluttering the same place in the air that she had always been.

Eliho landed his front feet back on the earth and proceeded to lay back down and again looked at Tephi.

"Yes my child, a gift." He said humbly.

Being overwhelmed by what had just happened, Tephi had a single tear slowly slip from the side of her eye, for what she saw in the flame was so very dear to her.

She flew towards Eliho, and wrapped her small arms around his huge neck. "Forgive me Eliho, for I did not know." Tephi said

Eliho replied. "My child there is no need for apologies."

Tephi flew back face to face with Eliho and looking into his eyes she felt a warm kindness and peace.

Eliho smiled at Tephi and spoke. "My gift is bringing life back to its purest state." With that he shrunk back down to a salamander right before her eyes, smiled at her and said. "I look forward to our next meeting Tephi." As he scurried away into the nearby forest.

Tephi turned with her mouth open to Dunkelwison. He smiled. "I told you he was a special friend."

Tephis mouth closed and a smile came across her face.

"Now Tephi. How did you end up here?" Dunkelwison asked.

"Well, when i got to the village I saw Eliho and after the flames burned out the next day i tried to show everyone how to regrow the village. But then I heard people questioning me and my voice cracked a few times and when I opened my mouth to sing nothing happened. Then they went back about sifting through the ashes trying to find their old things. I flew out of there unnoticed and continued flying wondering what had gone wrong until I ended up here."

"Hmmmmmm." Dunkelwison sighed, and then spoke. "What do you think went wrong?"

"Well." Tephi began. "That's what ive been thinking about. I was so excited to show my people everything that I've learned, and when the time came I was nervous. I started to listen to the people and focused more on them and what they were saying. Then tried to sing and nothing happened."

"Except for your voice cracking." Dunkelwison interrupted calmly.

"Yes." Tephi replied.

Dunkelwison smiled. Tephi was at a loss. "I don't understand what went wrong." She said saddened.

Dunkelwison spoke softly. "Doubt."

Tephi looked up and asked Dunkelwison. "What was that?"

Dunkelwison replied to Tephi. "My dear Tephi, when we focus on what others say about us and lose sight of our true nature, seeds get planted.

"Seeds?" Tephi questioned

"Yes Tephi." Dunkelwison spoke. "Just like the great oak that burnt that you helped grow back to life. It started as a seed. Certain conditions it had to have to grow big and tall. It needed sunlight, water, earth, wind to be able to grow big and tall. Then in a day all the time it had grown was taken away. See Tephi then you came along and with your beautiful heart song and helped it to regrow. The opposite can also happen. just as the seed was planted with you today."

Tephi interrupted and said "Doubt."

"Yes." Dunkelwison replied. "Doubt."

"If you choose to let go of your truth and start believing others your trueness will start to fade and slowly your heart song will no longer have its power. When seeds are planted it's our choice to decide if we want them to grow."

Tephi listened with an open heart and said. "I understand Dunkelwison. I just don't know if I can go back to the village."

"Hmmmm." Dunkelwison sighed and asked. "Why is that?"

"Because I'm afraid Dunkelwison." Tephi said lowering her eyes.

"Oh?" Dunkelwison said questioningly.

Tephi replied. "Yes, I'm afraid of what others will think and say, but more afraid of..." She paused then looked back up at Dunkelwison. "What if I can't sing again? What if?"

Dunkelwison interrupted. "Tephi stop." He sighed and spoke softly. "My dear you are giving roots to the seeds that others have sewn"

"How am I doing that?" Tephi asked.

"My dear little one." Dunkelwison spoke. "Fear, you gave it roots by being afraid, then the roots gained depth by your what ifs." "Tephi." He continued in a soft calming voice. "It's time for you to center yourself. Close your eyes little one. Think back to the oak. Watch yourself as you sing. What do you notice."

"The wind." Tephi replied. "It's sharing with me a powerful song."

"What else?" Dunkelwison prompted.

"I feel the trees heart pulsing through my hands. I feel it is still alive."

"What else?" Dunkelwison prompted again.

"Nothing." Tephi spoke. "I'm focused on the heart of the tree and singing the song."

Tephi opened her eyes. "I see now." She said peacefully. "I was so focused on what others would think and by doing so lost the focus of what I had known all along. Thank you Dunkelwison, thank you for always being here."

Smiling Dunkelwison replied. "Of course my dear Tephi, you are most welcome. I will always be here for you. Now my dear Tephi your village still needs you.

"I know." Tephi replied. She turned and started to fly back to the village. As she started off she could hear Dunkelwison say in the distance. "Show them what they have forgotten."

Flying back to the village she spoke aloud. "Grelos, Syllydidy, Delariah, Tulamar."

The wind answered in one voice. "Yesssss chilllld."

Tephi continued. "I need your help when I go back into the village. I need to remember all that I've learned and..." Tephi paused and spoke softly. "Be with me as i sing."

The wind spoke as one. "We most definitely will my child."

Tephi, feeling more determined and with a sense of peace neared the edge of the village. As she arrived she saw the fairies still searching trying to make new shelters out of old branches and twigs.

She said aloud to herself. "I don't think they'll listen."

The wind replied. "You're right Tephi the majority won't but the few who do will end up teaching all. Are you ready Tephi?" The wind asked.

Tephi spoke. "You'll be with me?"

"Of course our dear child." The wind concluded

With the wind on her side, she confidently flew back to the center of the charred village. Taking a deep breathe she landed on the tree where she had once been before. She knelt down and placed her hands on the center of the stump feeling it's beautiful heart still beating. While exhaling, the wind gusted up a swirl of ashes around her causing everyone to stop what they were doing and turn their attention to the center. When the ash settled they saw Tephi kneeling with her hands on the stump.

One spoke. "Oh great, Tephi is back. What's she going to do to help us now?" The crowd chuckled

Tephi heard the comment and dismissed the seed. She took a deep breath still focusing on the heart beat that she felt in her hands. Releasing her breath she started to sing. New life started to sprout from the stump as it grew taller and taller reaching towards the sky it once again encircled her and enclosed Tephi as part of the tree.

In seconds the tree was sprouting new buds and the leaves started to unfold. Tephi with her new wings, was seen flying out of the base of the tree where she had been seen kneeling on the stump.

Emerging from the tree she saw the older faires had turned away back to the building of their shelters not seeing the magic of the new beautiful tree.

She spoke softly to herself. "They don't see it." Before she could finish her train of thought she felt a tug on the hem of her skirt.

She looked down to see Ecargel one of the younger fairies. Ecargel's eyes were wide with astonishment.

Ecargel began to speak softly to Tephi. "How did you do that Tephi?"

Tephi lowered herself and looked into Ecargel's eyes. "Would you like to learn?" Tephi asked

Ecargel's eyes widened as she grabbed Tephi's hand

"Yes please, Tephi." Ecargel replied.

"Where was your house before the fire?" Tephi asked.

Ecargel flapping her wings flew Tephi to where her house once was.

They both landed on the stump of the tree, Tephi guided Ecargel to kneel with her and placed Ecargel's hands on the center of the tree.

Tephi spoke. "Close your eyes Ecargel and tell me what you notice?"

Ecargel placed her hands on the center of the stump, closed her eyes as tight as she could and felt the first buh bump.

She opened her eyes in excitement. "Tephi I felt it's heart beat. It's still! alive!" She exclaimed.

Tephi smiled and replied. "It very much is. Are you ready to awaken it?"

Ecargel nodded her head in excitement

Tephi guided. "Now close your eyes again and keep your hands where you felt its heartbeat."

Ecargel placed her hands back down. She could feel the buh bump, buh bump of the trees heart beat.

Tephi asked. "Do you feel its heart?"

Nodding with her eyes closed and hands on the stump Ecargel replied softly. "Yes."

Tephi guided. "Take a deep breath. One that fills you completely."

Ecargel took a very deep breath filling her entire body, as she started to exhale she softly and quietly started to sing a song

"I feel your heart within my hands
Grow grow grow again
Rise up and stand more than you were
Grow grow grow again
Voices in one that we will be
Grow grow grow again
With love from my heart, see that's the key
Grow grow grow again."

While Ecargel sang this song a little tree started sprouting up through her hands and soon was growing and encompassed her as part of the new tree.

Tephi fluttered up watching the new tree grow with a smile in her heart. Soon a branch shot out and new buds formed and the first one that unfurled held Ecargel.

Ecargel saw Tephi, and leaped off of the leaf and flew straight into Tephi wrapping her arms around her.

"Thank you Tephi." Ecargel said with tears in her eyes.

Tephi looked down returned her hug and replied. "Very welcome Ecargel." They fluttered down to the earth to look up at the new tree they noticed that the tree's color had changed to the deep purple and sky blue of the flames that ran through its bark.

Together Tephi and Ecargel reached out and placed their hands on the beautiful tree and thanked it. After a while of standing there connecting with it, Tephi turned and saw a multitude of the younger fairies flying over to the new tree.

Ecargel looked up to Tephi and spoke. "Teach them Tephi."

Tephi knelt down to look Ecargel face to face, placed Ecargel's hands in hers and replied with a question. "With your help?"

Ecargels eyes full of joy and hope smiled big and nodded her head up and down.

Soon a circle had formed around Tephi, Ecargel and the tree. The young fairies were amazed. One started to talk. "Ecargel what? how?" But couldn't find the words to complete a sentence.

Ecargel spoke. "You all know Tephi. She taught me how to do this."

All the young fairies were silent for a moment. Then one broke the silence. "Teach me!" The first exclaimed then another. "Teach me!" And another. "I want to learn!" Soon the whole crowd was agreeing about wanting to be taught.

Tephi's little heart smiled. A tear came to her eye. She heard the wind whisper. These are the few who will teach the many. Tephi's heart swelled with hope.

As the excitement quieted down Tephi spoke. "Ok, ok my young masters. Each of you fly to the trees where your homes were."

Tephi flew up into the sky where they all could hear her. She began. "Place your hands on the center of the tree, kneel down and close your eyes."

As each one did this she spoke again. "What do you notice?"

One spoke. "It's still alive." Another spoke. "I can feel its roots drinking water." Each relayed what they were sensing, Tephi smiled then continued. "Well done young masters. Now with your eyes closed take a deep breath in through your nose and then when you are ready, open your mouth.

The young fairies breathed in, Tephi felt the wind swirl as it went to embrace each one. The first opened her mouth and a beautiful song emerged. Then another opened and sang, and another sang, until the whole village was filled with a beautiful song each one different from the next.

While the little fairies sang from their hearts. The parents and elders stopped and looked up, and saw new trees springing forth right before their very eyes. Branches were shooting out and new leafs were unfurling. The first leaf held each one of the young faires.

Tephi flew higher over the canopy and spoke the names of the winds and thanked them for letting her be part of this. She descended back below the canopy and she saw the little fairies fly down from their leaves and hug the trees. Their parents flew to their children. You could hear the elders ask. "How is this possible?" Some others you could hear saying. "I just don't believe it." Yet some inquired. "How did you do this?"

Pretty soon the parents were listening to their children. They described all about the magic that each one went through.

Fluttering Tephi could hear the wind speak. "Thank you my dear for trusting. Your time here is finished. Are you ready for your next adventure?"

"Next adventure?" Tephi questioned

"Yes child." The wind answered. "A far grander and more spectacular journey awaits you."

Tephi smiled and replied. "Yes. I am."

Tephi turned to leave and as she started to fly away she was stopped by the elders. When they spoke they asked. "Tephi we don't understand this. How can we do this?"

Tephi replied to them smiling. "My dear friends I have to leave but you have a great teacher here in your midst." She motioned for Ecargel. Ecargel flew up to Tephi. Tephi took her hand and looked at her. "Will you teach them?" Tephi asked.

Ecargel's eyes filled with excitement nodded her head. Tephi looked back up to the elders and said. "She is a great teacher. She holds the answers that you seek."

With that, Tephi turned flapping both sets of wings and disappeared from their sight.

And as all good journeys come to an end, I leave you with this my friends: as you walk through the woods, be silent. Listen deeply with an open heart and if you are lucky you may just hear the songs that the fairies sing, and catch a glimpse of Tephi on her next adventure.

To hear Tephi's Waking song, please visit www. tephisjourney.com for your free download.

Printed in the United States
By Bookmasters